The Triplets Get Charmed

Read More
Trillium Sisters
Stories!

2: Bestie Day

Trillium Sisters

The Triplets Get Charmed

Laura Brown and Elly Kramer

Illustrated by Sarah Mensinga

PIXEL✛INK

PIXEL✚INK

Text copyright © 2021 by Laura Brown and Elly Kramer

Interior illustrations copyright © by TGM Development Corp.

All rights reserved

Pixel+Ink is a division of TGM Development Corp.

Printed and bound in April 2021 at Maple Press, York, PA, U.S.A.

Book design by Yaffa Jaskoll

www.pixelandinkbooks.com

Library of Congress Control Number: 2020943946

Hardcover ISBN 978-1-64595-014-1

Paperback ISBN 978-1-64595-015-8

eBook ISBN 978-1-64595-070-7

First Edition

1 3 5 7 9 10 8 6 4 2

For Doug, David, Richard, and Sarah,
my own magic charms. —L.B.

For Lauren, sister power, forever! —E.K.

CHAPTER 1

Emmy woke up as the morning sun shone brightly through the window of the tree house. She stretched in her hammock, reaching in opposite directions with her fingers and toes and, *whoops!* She accidentally woke her pet bear cub, Claw, who'd been sound asleep next to her.

Emmy smiled at Claw. Then, putting her finger to her lips, she swung her legs gently to the floor. She didn't want to wake her sisters, Giselle and Clare, who were still asleep in their own hammocks.

But Claw wasn't good at being quiet. *Tap, tap, thud* went Claw as her front paws, then her bottom, hit the floor.

Giselle shot straight up in her hammock. "Whatzat?" she said.

Clare rubbed her eyes. "Hello?" she said.

"Oh, pine cones!" said Emmy. "Sorry, we woke you!"

Giselle and Clare climbed out of their hammocks, gently putting their own pets, an eaglet named

Soar and a wolf pup named Fluffy, on the floor. They grinned at Emmy. No one minded being woken on such a special day.

"Happy Founding Day!" they all cried at once. Then, the three sisters ran and threw their arms around one another in a terrifically tight triplet hug.

The pets scurried over, and the sisters scooped them up into the hug, too.

Founding Day was their family's favorite holiday. Eight years ago on this very day, babies Emmy, Clare, and Giselle had been found in the forest by their father.

Their dad, Dr. J.A., was a veterinarian who took care of all the animals who lived on the mountain. But it got a little lonely in the

tree house. Trillville, the village where most people on the mountain lived, was a good fifteen minutes away by zip line.

That's why it had seemed almost magical when he'd found the triplets. Ever since that day, the family had celebrated Founding Day like other families celebrated birthdays. On Founding Day, they spent the day together, playing games and decorating the tree house. And Dad always made a special dinner with their favorites—daisy juice and trillium cupcakes.

"What should we play first?" asked Giselle.

"We always start Founding Day with a game of hide-and-find," said Clare.

"Perfect! Let's go hide," said Giselle.

"But Dad is on morning rounds, checking

all the animals. There's no reason to hide until he can find us," said Emmy.

"I've got an idea!" said Clare. "Let's make trillium pancakes and decorate the table with paper trillium flowers. We'll surprise Dad with a special Founding Day breakfast."

Emmy smiled at her sister. Clare had a passion for pretty. She especially loved the wildflowers that grew all over the mountain. Trilliums were her favorite. With three petals, the trillium was a triplet, just like Clare, Giselle, and Emmy were. That's why they called each other "Trills."

"Trilltastic idea, sis," said Emmy. "But do you think we have time to make it all before Dad gets back?"

"I'll stand in the yard," said Clare. "If Dad comes, I'll distract him while you two get everything ready!" Clare grabbed her jacket and headed to the slide that ran from the top of the tree house into the yard. "Woohoo!"

she cried as she slid down. She flew into the yard and headed for the gate.

Back in the kitchen, Emmy sat at the table making paper trillium flowers from white and pink construction paper. Giselle got out ingredients for the pancake batter. "Flour, honey, butter, eggs, milk . . ." said Giselle. "Am I forgetting anything?"

"Just this!" said Emmy. She lifted a skillet shaped like three connected petals off its hook. Can't make trillium pancakes without the trillium pan!"

"*Grrrh-huh!*" agreed Claw.

"*Ahoo!*" howled Fluffy, drooling.

"*Yip, yip!*" said Soar as she bounced up and down.

"Don't worry, mini'mals." Giselle giggled.

"You can lick the bowl."

"Mini'mals" was the nickname the girls had given their pets when they were mini baby animals. Dr. J.A. thought the name was clever, and it had stuck.

Giselle mixed the pancake batter. Then she covered the bowl and put it in the fridge to stay cold. As Emmy stood up to lay paper flowers on each plate, she was almost knocked over by their little brother, Zee, who bounded in.

"Whoa! Morning, Zee!" said Emmy.

"I don't see Zee," said Giselle. "Just a lot of hair."

Zee pushed aside his long blond bangs and ran to Giselle. "Here I am, Gelly!" he cried.

"Ya got me," laughed Giselle. She caught him under

the arms and spun him around.

The kitchen door opened, and Clare stepped inside. "No sign of Dad yet," she said. "How are the trillium pancakes coming?"

"Trillium pancakes?" said Zee.

"We're making Breakfast Surprise for Dad," said Clare. "It's Founding Day!"

"Oh, yeah!" said Zee, bouncing up and down. "I love surprises!"

"Ahoo!" howled Fluffy. Breakfast sounded pretty good, too.

"The pancake batter is ready. Let's go hide

so Dad can find us when he finishes rounds," said Giselle.

She headed for the ladder that connected the kitchen to the upper floors of the tree house, but Zee scrambled over to the big double windows in the family room. He tucked himself behind the curtains.

"Good spot!" said Clare.

"Stay quiet and Dad will never find you," said Emmy.

The girls scooped up the mini'mals and climbed the ladder to the third floor. They needed a place big enough for the three of them, and it had to be good! They didn't want Dad pretending he couldn't find them like he had when they were little.

As they piled into their bedroom, Giselle

pointed up. "Let's climb to the top of my climbing wall. If we don't make a peep, Dad won't think to look up. We'll be over his head and he'll never know it!"

The girls scrambled up the climbing wall that Dr. J.A. had built. It covered an entire wall in their room and was at least fifteen feet high. From the top pegs, you could turn your head and look out the window to see the mountainside below. Dad liked to joke it was a real bird's-eye view.

"Awesome!" said Emmy. "Dad will never find us here!"

"*Grrr!*" said Claw from the floor, wiggling her bottom back and forth.

"Oh, sour flowers!" said Clare. "We forgot

the minis. When Dad sees them, he'll know we're here."

They girls climbed back down and led their pets into the craft room next door. Emmy eyed the huge bins that lined the walls.

"Are you thinking what I'm thinking?" said Emmy.

"Bull's-eye," said Giselle as she removed colored paper and markers from a bin. "We'll hide in the empty bins . . ."

". . . *with* the minis!" finished Emmy.

"Now you're getting crafty!" said Clare.

Giggling, the sisters crawled into the bins, pulled their pets onto their laps, and waited.

CHAPTER 2

Dr. J.A. climbed the mountain path, humming as he finished his morning rounds. The air smelled fresh, the sun warmed his arms, and a slight breeze tickled his skin. He figured the kids were still asleep. Mrs. Lilienstern, their next-door neighbor, was at home should they need anything before he got back.

He passed squirrels scurrying up a tree

and bluebirds flitting from branch to branch. He saw Bruce the Moose munching moss. He made checkmarks against each animal's name on his clipboard, where he recorded their status. The forest sure looked healthy today!

Dr. J.A. stopped at the Grand Oak Tree, and the trillium patch that grew beneath its leafy branches. This was his favorite spot in the forest because it was here that he'd found his daughters eight years ago. The girls had even made a wooden plaque to mark the spot. Staked in the ground, it read: FOR DR. J.A., OUR DAD, WHO FOUND US HERE! HE IS JUST AWESOME!

He rested on the soft earth as the

memories rushed back. He had been inspecting the mountain that morning like always, when he'd heard a cry. He had turned toward the sound. Was he seeing right? There, nestled in the patch, were three babies! Each had a small animal by their side: a baby bear, a wolf pup, and an eaglet. The animals were curled against the girls, trying to keep them warm, but they were no match for the crisp morning air. The girls were shivering.

Dr. J.A. had snapped into action, scooping the babies up and zooming through the forest. He'd raced through the meadow and hopped from stone to stone across the stream to the tree house, where he burst into the family room. Snatching a feather blanket, he'd bundled the girls up and watched, relieved, as they stopped shivering. Once warmed, the animals had nestled their heads onto his lap as if to say thank you.

He had officially adopted the girls a year later as soon as the town clerk assured him that no blood relative could be located. But the girls had been his family from the moment he had laid eyes on them.

Dr. J.A. let out a happy sigh and stood back up. He was so proud of how his girls had begun to mature and work together, like the team he'd always hoped they'd be! Just last week, Clare had forgotten to put away the glitter glue and the mini'mals had tracked sparkly paw prints all over the tree house. But instead of bickering over whose fault it was, the girls had cleaned up the mess together, lickety-split.

He glanced at his watch. It was time to get home and celebrate Founding Day! He started to head down the mountain, but his foot caught on something and he fell face-first into the flowers.

"Aww, maple sugar!" he said.

But when he scanned the ground to see what he'd tripped over, instead of a branch or a rock, he saw that a whole patch of trillium flowers had been uprooted. It looked like someone had yanked them up, and then left them there to wither away.

He had to do something, and fast. He

knelt down to examine the plants' roots. They were still moist, which was a good sign. With luck, he could save these precious trilliums, but he'd need help. Just as he had eight years before, Dr. J.A. took a deep breath and sprinted down the mountain toward home.

CHAPTER 3

"Girls! Zee!" he cried as he ran toward home. "Code Green! Code Green!"

In the tree house, Emmy leapt out of the bin where she'd been hiding. "Trills, did you hear that?"

"Yup! This is *not* the time for hide-and-find," said Giselle. "Stay put, mini'mals."

"Is that Daddy?" called Zee from downstairs. "Should I come out?"

"Abso-trilly!" yelled Clare.

"I'm coming for ya, Zee," said Emmy as she made for the ladder.

"Trills, in the yard, in three!" called Giselle. She whooshed down the slide.

"Two!" Clare followed her.

"One!" Emmy bolted out the kitchen door and down the steps holding Zee by the hand.

The kids made it to the yard just as Dr. J.A. pushed open the wooden gate. He had run so fast, he had to gulp breaths of air before he could speak.

"Dad, what's the Code Green?!" said Clare.

"There's trillium trouble," said Dr. J.A. "C'mon!"

"On the triple!" cried Emmy.

Dr. J.A. grabbed some gardening tools,

and they all ran out of the yard and back up the path as fast as they could. Giselle arrived first and gasped. "Dad! Who hurt our trilliums?"

"Who would *want* to?" said Clare. "They're the most beautiful flowers on the mountain."

"And on Founding Day!" said Emmy. "This is making me so sad." She looked like she might cry.

"Don't worry, Em," said Zee. "We can fix them!" He hugged her waist and then dropped to his knees, scratching at the soil with his little fingers.

"Good idea, Zee," said Dr. J.A. "We need to replant the flowers, but we have to be careful not to harm the roots." He knelt beside his son and dug a neat hole in between two flowers with a trowel. "See? Now put the roots and then the flower gently into the hole."

"Now dirt, Daddy?" said Zee.

"Yup, fill up the hole and pat dirt all around to support the stem."

The family got to work. Zee and Emmy replanted the trilliums while Clare and Giselle fetched water from the stream. They were all so focused, only the buzz of the bees could be heard.

When they were finally finished, they were covered in dirt. Zee even had mud in his hair! But the flowers stood upright once again, petals opening toward the sun that filtered down through the oak tree's leaves.

"I hope it works," said Emmy. She gently stroked a petal.

"You and me both," said Dr. J.A. He stood, frowning. They had done their best, but he still felt uneasy. The patch where he'd found his girls was damaged.

"Dad," called Giselle swinging from a branch on the oak tree. "Now that the flowers are replanted, remember, it's *Founding Day*!" She landed next to him.

"Of course! I'm sorry. The Code Green distracted me. Happy Founding Day!" He hugged them all. "Let's go celebrate."

"Guess what?" said Clare. "This year, *we're* going to surprise *you*!"

"I love surprises!" said Zee as he jumped up and down. Giselle ran up and tickled him from behind.

"Gelly, not *that* kind of surprise!" laughed Zee. "Stop!"

"Hey! Should we race home?!" said Giselle. "Who's in?"

"Me!" they all cried.

"In three . . ." began Emmy.

"Two-One!" squealed Zee. He took off down the trail as the girls raced after him.

CHAPTER 4

Giselle made it home first, as usual. She crouched behind a bush with the garden hose waiting for the others.

When Clare ran into the yard, Giselle doused her. "Yaah!" Clare giggled as the dirt washed off her.

"Ahhh!" yelled Emmy as the spray hit her, too.

Zee ran in and jumped in front of the hose. "Get me! Get me!"

Giselle squirted him from top to bottom.

"More!" laughed Zee.

"Maybe later," said Emmy. She shut off the hose. "We can't do Breakfast Surprise if we're muddy and soaking wet."

"Ooo, the surprise!" said Zee. "Where's Daddy?"

"He's still walking back," said Giselle.

"Let's change so we're ready when he gets here," said Clare.

They headed inside, but Emmy lingered in the yard.

"Be up in a sec," she said. She spotted Dr. J.A. slowly winding down the path. He seemed lost in thought. She pushed open the gate. "Dad, you okay?"

Dr. J.A. looked up and smiled. "Sure, honey. I'm fine. I just can't stop wondering . . . who yanked up those trilliums—and why?"

"I know," said Emmy. "It doesn't make sense. Actually, there's a bunch of stuff I've been wondering about."

"Ask away," said her dad.

She brought her father under the tree

house to the chart where they'd tracked their heights since they were little. "Look, Dad. Giselle, Clare, and I grow every year."

"I'd worry if you shrank!" said Dr. J.A.

"Ba-dum-ba!" they said together.

"Seriously though," continued Emmy. "Shouldn't the mini'mals be getting taller, too? Claw's eight like us, but she's still the size of a baby cub. It doesn't make sense."

Dr. J.A. frowned. That was a mystery he'd noodled on for years. He hadn't realized the girls thought about it, too. His daughters were getting older. Maybe they were ready to hear the *entire* Founding Day story.

The kitchen door slammed and Clare, Giselle, and Zee skipped into the yard.

"Man, have we got a treat for *you*, Dad!" said Clare.

"To the kitchen!" said Giselle.

But Dr. J.A. hesitated. "Thanks," he said. "But before we go inside, there's something I want to tell you."

"Dad's *really* worried about the trillium patch," explained Emmy.

"But we fixed the flowers, Daddy!" said Zee.

"We did, buddy," said Dr. J.A. "It's something else, something I don't know how to fix."

"We can help, Dad!" said Clare. She took his hand and pulled him down to the grass. "Spill," she said.

Dr. J.A. raised a confused eyebrow.

"Tell us! Everything!" she said.

He took a deep breath. "Kids, there's more to the Founding Day story than I've shared with you," he began.

"More?" said Giselle.

"Yep. Some strange things happened the day I found you. I never told you because . . . well . . ." He took his glasses off and rubbed his eyes. "I don't understand it all myself."

Emmy took his hand. "That's okay, Dad. You always say 'You don't have to understand things for them to be true.'"

"Right, Em," said Dr. J.A. "And this is something I definitely don't understand."

The Trills stared at their dad. He looked so serious, even troubled. Breakfast would have to wait.

CHAPTER 5

They sat in the cool grass. Dr. J.A. stroked Fluffy. "You see how friendly and gentle Fluffy is right now? Well, when I first found you girls in the trillium patch, the mini'mals weren't friendly at all."

"These cuties?" said Emmy. She cupped Claw's chin and the bear cub licked her face.

"That's right. Claw growled every time I

tried to pick you up," said Dr. J.A.

"What about Soar? She *can't* growl," said Giselle.

"No, but she beat her wings whenever I tried to get near you babies!" Dr. J.A. explained. "You were shivering and it was so cold out."

"So what'd you do, Dad?" asked Clare.

"I noticed that the mini'mals were guarding not only you girls, but also a large white trillium in the middle of the patch. Every time I came close to it, they circled the flower and bared their teeth."

"But they were babies, Daddy!" said Zee.

"True, but baby wolf teeth are still pretty sharp! I knew I needed to calm them. So I took everything out of my daypack and let them sniff it all."

"Like we do with the forest animals? So they'd get used to your scent?" asked Emmy.

"Exactly, Em!" said Dr. J.A. "And I had some granola. I sprinkled it on the ground. After the minis gobbled it up, they trusted me."

"How could you tell?" said Giselle.

"They let me near the big white trillium flower. As I got close to the flower to inspect it, the strangest thing happened!"

"What, Daddy, what?!" said Zee.

"The trillium. It . . ." Dr. J.A. shook his head. "Well, it glowed!" he said softly.

"Really?!" said Clare.

"Yes!" said Dr. J.A. "I was so surprised, I leaned over to touch it."

"What'd it feel like?" said Giselle.

"I don't know, because then, things got even stranger!" said Dr. J.A.

Zee's mouth hung open. "What happened?!"

"The trillium burst into a cloud of sparkly dust!" Dr. J.A. exclaimed.

Giselle looked at her dad. Then, she started to laugh. "You had me for a sec! Sparkly dust—c'mon!"

The doctor looked evenly at his daughter. "I know it sounds crazy, but I'm not kidding. The flower disintegrated into a cloud of sparkles!"

Everyone was quiet.

He continued. "When the dust finally cleared, something incredible lay in place of the flower. Something I've been keeping for you girls in the tree house ever since."

The Trills stared at their father. They didn't know what to say.

"And now," their father said, "you are old enough to take good care of them."

Dr. J.A. stood and walked to the trunk of the tree house, then wiggled into the narrow space between the tree and the slide. He pointed to a knot in the trunk, hidden behind the slide.

"Is that a hole?" said Clare.

"I never knew that was there!" exclaimed Giselle.

"Your dad still has a few surprises up his sleeve!" said Dr. J.A.

"I love surprises!" said Zee.

"Well, get ready for a big one!" The doctor reached into the knot. His arm went so deep, the girls could see only his shoulder.

"No way!" said Emmy.

"There's stuff in the hole?!" said Clare.

"Cool! Can *I* hide in the hole?" Zee bounced up and down.

Dr. J.A laughed. "Absolutely not. The hole is for trinkets, not small boys."

"Do you need help, Dad?" asked Emmy.

"Nope, almost got it," said Dr. J.A, grunting. He stretched a little farther, then pulled out an old cardboard box.

"Happy Founding Day," he said as he gingerly lifted a bundle wrapped in tissue paper from the box. "First, for Zee." Dr. J.A. pulled a toy metal race car—pocket-sized—from the first layer of the bundle. Dad had collected race cars as a boy, and he was slowly handing them down to Zee. "This one was always my favorite."

"A hot rod with thunderbolts!" cried Zee. "I'm gonna call it *Boom*!"

"Boom's gonna zoom!" said Dr. J.A.

"Can I go race it, Daddy?" Zee asked. He ran off before Dr. J.A. could answer.

The doctor turned back to the triplets. Then, he slowly unwound the rest of the tissue paper, revealing three trillium petal

charms:
one blue,
one green,
and one pink. They
were the exact shape and

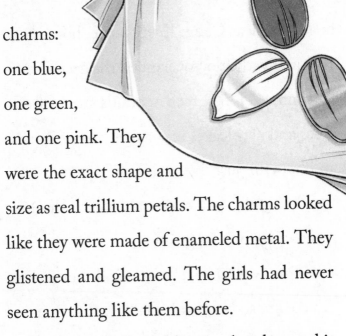

size as real trillium petals. The charms looked like they were made of enameled metal. They glistened and gleamed. The girls had never seen anything like them before.

Dr. J.A. lifted the blue petal and passed it to Giselle. "You're as strong and fearless as the bold blue of this charm. That's how I know it was meant for you."

Next, he held up a hot pink charm, and laid it in Clare's palm, wrapping her fingers around it. "A charm this bold and bright must be for my dear Clare. Keep it safe, honey."

Finally, the doctor handed the green petal to Emmy. "This green reminds me of fresh grass and new leaves in spring—sweet, warm, and hopeful, just like you, Em."

The girls marveled at their charms, speechless, for a long time.

Clare was the first to find her voice. "These are so beautiful, Dad!"

"Yes, thanks, Dad. We love them," said Emmy.

"Vroooom! Ba-*BOOM*!" The special moment was interrupted by Zee. "Daddy, guess what's in the kitchen!" he called.

"Hold up, little bro," Giselle called. "It's a surprise, remember?"

She turned back to Dr. J.A. "Dad, these charms are so cool. But we have a treat for you, too. Maybe you should see it before Zee ruins the surprise!"

"Close your eyes," said Clare.

After the long morning, Dr. J.A. was happy to do just that. He smiled as his daughters led him inside.

CHAPTER 6

Dr. J.A.'s eyes went wide as he took in the table decorated so beautifully with trilliums.

"We made a pancake Breakfast Surprise," said Giselle.

"Surprise!!" said Zee.

"This looks amazing!" said Dr. J.A. "Trills, why don't you put your charms away while I clean up from the planting. Then, we'll eat."

The girls clambered up the ladder to their bedroom. "We have to find a safe spot for these precious charms," said Clare. "Should we lock them in our jewelry box?"

"No, we can't leave them there!" Giselle replied.

"Why not? It's perfect," said Clare a little huffily.

Emmy looked at Giselle thoughtfully. "I think Giselle doesn't want to leave the charms anywhere."

"That *is* what I mean," Giselle said, throwing her arms up in the air. "We've already been separated from them for eight years!"

"True," Clare agreed as she looked out the window. She clapped her hands. "Dancing daisies! What if we made them into jewelry? That way, the charms will be with us wherever we go!"

"That's a great idea!" said Emmy. "Right, Giselle?"

Giselle shrugged. "Guess that would work," she said.

That was good enough for Clare. She hurried into the craft room and plucked supplies off the shelves—colored lanyard, silver wire, glue. Emmy placed them on the wooden picnic table in the center of the room and handed Giselle a bright blue lanyard. Giselle took it with a smile, and the girls got to work.

"Check it out!" Giselle said a little

while later, holding up a woven anklet with the blue petal glinting at its center. "Now I can wear my charm while I'm running through the forest!"

Clare, who had been allowed to pierce her ears on their seventh Founding Day, twisted wire around her petal, making a dangly earring. The hot pink charm moved softly against her cheek as she wagged her head back and forth. "How's *this* for fashion forward?!" she asked her sisters.

Emmy braided colored lanyard into a chain for her neck and hung her charm from it. "I want mine close to my heart," she said.

The girls couldn't wait to show Dad their

charm jewelry, but as they headed downstairs, they saw he was dressed for the forest, not breakfast. Mrs. Lilienstern stood with one foot in the doorway.

"Girls, I'm *so* sorry," Dad said as he pulled on his daypack. "Bruce the Moose has a plastic bag tangled around his antlers."

"Yes!" continued Mrs. Lilienstern. "He can't see where he's going! The poor dear is going to hurt himself. And he's trampling everything in his path. I'm off to protect the saplings!" With that, she ran out the door.

"The pancakes will have to wait a little longer," said Dr. J.A.

"But my tummy is empty, Daddy!" said Zee. He patted it for effect.

"I had time to make snacks," said their dad. On the counter were granola bars and orange slices on a plate. "Enjoy! I'll be back when Bruce the Moose is loose," he said. He giggled at his own rhyme and walked out the door.

CHAPTER 7

Zee made a beeline for the snacks, but the girls suddenly didn't feel hungry. They sat quietly at the table, staring at their plates.

"I know Dad has important things to do, but he's missing a lot of Founding Day," said Giselle.

"Yeah, it's not as fun as it usually is," Clare agreed.

Emmy fiddled with her charm and stared out the window. Finally, she forced her mouth into a small smile and looked at her sisters. "Trills, even though Founding Day didn't start the way we wanted, it hasn't been all bad. Maybe if we think about the good parts, we'll feel better."

"What good parts?" said Clare, tracing a circle on the tabletop.

"Well, we *did* save the trillium patch," said Emmy.

"Yeah," Giselle said, sitting a little straighter. "And Dad decided we're grown up enough to be trusted with these charms."

Clare smiled and touched her new earring. "He's proud of us."

"That's the best part!" said Emmy.

Clare jumped to her feet. "Let's make Dad's Breakfast Surprise even better!" said Clare. "Chocolate is Dad's favorite. We can add chocolate chips to the batter!"

"Yum!" said Zee.

Emmy opened the cabinet to get the chocolate chips.

"Wait," said Giselle. "Dad loves strawberries,

too. We should pick some and put them on the pancakes. He'll like that better."

"No," said Clare. "Dad likes chocolate way better than strawberry." She started adding chocolate chips to the batter.

"Wrong!" Giselle countered, her voice growing louder. She grabbed the bowl of batter. "Strawberry is his favorite. He told me so."

"Did not!" said Clare.

"Did too!" said Giselle.

"Whoa!" said Emmy. "He loves chocolate *and* strawberries. So, how about—"

Giselle and Clare looked at each other, and then at Emmy.

"Choco-strawberry!" they all said at the same time.

"Choco-YUM!" said Zee, jumping up and down.

They just needed some strawberries. Emmy grabbed a wicker basket.

Zee bounced over to her. "Can I pick the strawberries, Em? Can I? Can I?"

She tousled his hair. "Zee, you know you can't go by yourself, but you *can* come with me."

Zee was out the door in a flash.

"Wait for me!" Emmy called. She whistled for Claw and together they ran after Zee.

CHAPTER 8

Emmy caught up with Zee and grabbed his hand. "Zee, you can't run off by yourself! You could get lost!"

"*Grr-huh!*" Claw gave a low deep growl.

"Sorry, Em. I'm just so excited!" said Zee. He grinned, gap-toothed, at her.

"Me too," she said. "But we have to stay *together*, okay?"

"Okay," said Zee.

As they walked through the forest, Emmy pointed to the plumpest berries and Zee ducked down to pop them off the stems. Their basket was half full when they heard rushing water.

"That's noisy!" shouted Zee.

"Yep, the snowcap on top of the mountain is melting. See?" said Emmy. She angled him so he could see all the water rushing down the mountainside into the river.

"Whoa! Can we wade in a little?" he asked.

"Not today, Zee. The river's rough because of all the snowmelt," Emmy explained.

"Aww!" said Zee. He shuffled down the path a little, but then he smiled. "Em! Look at those!" He pointed with both arms to a bridge that crossed the river. Strawberries were growing right up to the edge. "Mega-berries!"

"They *are* big!" said Emmy.

"Let's get some!" said Zee.

"Sure," said Emmy. She crouched down over her shoes. "Just hold on a sec. My laces are loose."

But all Zee heard was 'Sure,' and he took off.

"Ahoo!" went Claw.

"Almost done," said Emmy.

"AHOO!" Claw howled.

Emmy looked up. Zee wasn't there! He was on the bridge, leaning over the railing on tippy-toes to snag a huge strawberry!

"Zee, no!" yelled Emmy. She ran toward the bridge, her heart beating so loud it drummed in her ears.

But Zee didn't hear her. He leaned forward a little more, pressing his thighs on the top of the railing. "Emmy, look!" he cried. He whipped around to show Emmy his prize. But he was off-balance. He tipped over the railing and fell toward the water.

"Ahhh!" he cried.

Emmy raced onto the bridge and heard a sickly splash. She leaned over the railing, desperately searching the water for Zee. He popped up to the surface, treading water. She gasped with relief. *Thank goodness Dad taught us all to swim so young!*

A small log floated by. "Zee, grab the log!" she cried.

He threw both arms over it.

"Good! Now can you pull yourself on top of it?" she yelled.

Zee struggled, but finally got a leg over the log, too. He sat on it upright, like it was a horse. But the current was pushing the log downstream. It wouldn't be long before Zee was swept downriver. Emmy looked around frantically for some way to help him.

"Zee, grab those!" said Emmy. She pointed to some vines that hung from a tree branch over the water. They were twisted like a rope and dangled above Zee's head. He reached up and wrapped his little hands around them.

"Great job! Now, hold tight! I'm coming!" called Emmy. She raced to the path that led to the riverbank. "Claw, get help!" she yelled. But the little bear was already gone. Emmy knew Claw was well on her way home to do just that.

CHAPTER 9

Clare and Giselle lounged at the kitchen table, admiring their new jewelry and waiting for Emmy and Zee to return with the strawberries.

"I just can't *believe* these charms came from a trillium flower," said Giselle. "Do you think Dad made that part up?"

"Nuh-uh. Dad knows we're too old for fairy tales," said Clare.

"How about flower tales?" said Giselle.

Clare giggled. "Seriously, if the charms didn't come from the flower, where *did* they come from?"

"I haven't figured that out yet," said Giselle.

"Well, I'm with Dad," said Clare, "Just because you can't understand something, doesn't mean it isn't true."

"I guess," said Giselle.

Suddenly, Soar started to flap her wings fast. Fluffy's ears pricked up and he ran back and forth from the girls to the door, whining.

"What is it, Fluff?" said Clare. He nudged her toward the door with his snout.

Clare opened the door, and Fluffy charged down the steps just as Claw arrived at the backyard gate. *"AHOOOOO!"* It sounded like a moan.

"Where's Emmy?" cried Giselle.

Claw stood on her hind legs and bellowed, *"AHOOOOO!!"*

"Something's wrong!" yelled Clare.

Claw turned and raced back toward the forest with Giselle and Fluffy close behind. Clare and Soar ran after them, trying to keep up. The group tore through the forest until they reached the fork where the path split, one trail leading to the bridge and the other descending to the river.

Here, Claw stood on her hind legs, whining and trembling, unsure where to go.

"Where are they?" cried Giselle.

Nose to the ground, Fluffy raced in circles and then bounded on to the bridge. There, he leapt up, front paws on the railing, and barked furiously at the raging river below.

"They're in the river?!" cried Clare.

"AHOOOO!" howled Claw.

"C'mon!" cried Giselle. They sprinted down the river path. Overgrown plants and vines scratched at their arms, but they didn't notice. All they could hear was the rushing water.

"Emmy!" cried Giselle.

"Zee!" yelled Clare.

"There they are!!" shouted Giselle.

Zee was straddling a log in the middle of the river. It bucked as the wind picked up, making the water run faster. Emmy was waist deep in the river, trying to get to Zee.

"Giselle! Help us!" Zee cried.

Giselle raced into the water to reach Emmy. The current was so strong, Giselle had to dig her heels into the muck to stay upright. "Em! Come back!" she yelled over the rushing water.

"Nooo! I have to get Zee!" cried Emmy.

Giselle reached Emmy, grabbed her with both arms, and brought her out of the river. Tears streamed down Emmy's face.

"Em, we'll save Zee! But we need something to pull him in," said Clare.

They scoured the shore frantically. Giselle looked anxiously at those spindly vines her little brother was holding on to. She didn't want to think about what might happen if they gave way.

CHAPTER 10

Back in the forest, Dr. J.A. spotted Bruce the Moose. A plastic bag was draped across his antlers and hung down over his eyes. The doctor made soothing sounds before quickly removing the plastic bag and pocketing it. Bruce was so relieved, he licked Dr. J.A. all over with his big tongue.

"Thanks, Bruce. But I showered this morning," said Dr. J.A.

The big moose leaned his body against him in what felt like a moose hug.

"Glad I could help, buddy," said Dr. J.A. He fed Bruce some moss he'd dug up on his way over. When Bruce finished, Dr. J.A. gently shooed him back toward the thick forest. With a tip of his enormous head, Bruce shuffled back into the bushes.

As Dr. J.A. followed the trail back toward the tree house, he noticed ripe strawberries along the way. *These would be delicious with the Trills' Founding Day pancakes. Maybe with a little chocolate.* He pulled the plastic bag from his pocket and began to fill it with the red, juicy gems.

Then, his eye caught another patch of even bigger berries by the bridge. He headed that way, whistling, imagining dropping the sliced berries into the pancake batter.

But as he stepped onto the bridge, he did a double take. There were kids below and one was in the river! *Don't they know the snowcap is melting?!* He tucked the bag into his jacket and rushed down the path.

CHAPTER 11

The wind had kicked up, whipping the current even faster. It pushed Zee's log harder.

Snap! One of the vines broke.

"Ahhh!" screamed Zee.

"Hang on!" cried Emmy.

"Look!" called Clare. She pointed to a long branch hidden in the underbrush. "Can we reach him with that?"

Giselle raced over and they tugged at the branch as hard as they could.

"It . . . won't . . . budge," said Giselle as she pulled with all her might.

"We need something else! Think, think!" said Clare.

"Wait! There are three of us!" said Emmy.

"Yes! We'll hold hands and stretch to get him!" said Clare.

"Like a human chain?" asked Giselle.

"Exactly!" said Emmy.

Clare dug her heels into the shore like an anchor and grabbed Emmy's hand. Giselle held Emmy's other hand, and the two girls rushed into the water. Since she was the farthest out, Giselle leaned toward Zee. She was close enough that her fingertips just brushed the log.

"Lean farther!" Giselle called to her sisters. The Trills stepped as wide as they could and stretched until their sides ached. Giselle grabbed for the log again. Her fingertips were closing around the end of it, when a wave jostled it away. "No!" she cried.

"Help!" pleaded Zee. "I can't hold on any more!" He started to cry.

"Zee!" called Emmy. "Do *not* let go! We'll get you, I promise!"

"O . . . kay . . . Em . . . my," said Zee between sobs.

Emmy was looking around frantically, when Claw head-butted her in her calf. "The minis, of course! Claw can be the anchor to our chain and give us the extra length we need to reach Zee!" she cried.

Claw dug her hind feet into the ground and, holding onto the bear, Clare was able to step farther into the water. The sisters stretched out again toward their little brother. They were *so* close. Giselle was able to grab the underside of the log.

"Got it!" she exclaimed. She was breathing so hard, she could hardly get the words out.

Even though Emmy's

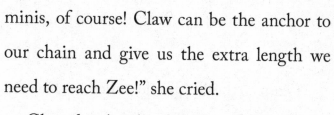
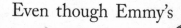

muscles were screaming, she held on. But then a big wave bumped the log up, and it came down hard into the frothing water, pushing Giselle's hand away. Then *snap!* Another vine broke.

"Aaahhhh!" cried Zee. There was only one vine left.

Emmy felt a sob rise in her throat. She couldn't let it out and scare Zee. Then suddenly, her hand flew to her neck.

"Wait . . . what?!" she cried. On her neck, she could feel that her green charm wasn't lying flat anymore. It had risen

off her chest and was hovering in the air! It strained, like a magnet, toward Clare's pink charm! "Trills, look!"

Then the two charms popped out of the jewlery and flew toward one another, hovering in the air!

"Trills, your charms are glowing, just like Dad said!" exclaimed Giselle.

In one smooth move, Giselle retrieved her blue charm from her anklet. It, too, was glowing. It whizzed toward the other two charms already in the air.

Zoom! The three charms shot together! They became one large, seamless, glowing trillium flower charm! Then, the flower charm fired off a massive flash of light. And *whoosh!* The mini'mals were transformed into a mighty eagle, a huge bear, and a muscular wolf!

Finally, with an even louder *fwomp,* the entire forest shimmered, and the girls were transformed, too! Standing on the bank of the river dressed in fierce outfits, they now looked like warriors, strong, united, and unstoppable!

CHAPTER 12

Before they could think about what had just happened, Dr. J.A. came running toward the river. "Hold on, son. I'm coming!" he cried as he dove headfirst into the rushing river.

Giselle charged back into the water, too. The doctor broke the surface a few feet downstream from Zee. He swam against the waves, but the current was too strong. It was pushing him away.

Giselle though, dove into the water and swam powerfully against the current toward her brother. *I would never have been able to do that before! It's like I have super strength.*

"Girls, what is going *on*?!" called Dr. J.A. "How is Giselle swimming like that?"

"Don't know, but I'm coming for you, Dad!" cried Emmy. She ran down the shore after her father.

"No, I'll be fine!" he called. "Help Giselle!" Treading furiously, Dr. J.A. pulled the plastic bag from his pocket. He held it by the handles and threw it up over his head.

As the strawberries sailed out, the bag filled with air. He quickly knotted it so the air couldn't escape. Then, he leaned on the inflated bag like a life preserver, and let the water push him safely downstream.

Clare, meanwhile, was watching the last vine that Zee was holding on to. Not just watching—her vision had zoomed in on the vines and she could see they were about to tear apart. She rubbed her eyes. *How can I see that from so far away?* She shouted, "Trills, time's up! The last vine is gonna break!"

Giselle had almost reached her brother. One last stroke, and she was able to wrap her arm over Zee's log. "Zee—"

But then, *snap!* The last vine broke and

the log was sucked into a section of water swirling around and around in a circle. The log began to spin, too!

"Ahhh!!" cried Zee. He fell forward, his little arms hugging the log tight as it spun, throwing Giselle off.

"GRRRR!" Claw's roar shook the forest. Transformed, she was the largest bear Emmy had ever seen.

"Yes, Claw! Go!" cried Emmy as Claw splashed into the river focused on helping.

"Blegh!" coughed Giselle. She surfaced near the log, spitting up water.

"Claw's coming, Giselle!" cried Clare. Claw bounded farther into the river, and Giselle managed to climb onto her back.

They moved over to where Zee was desperately holding onto the spinning log. Giselle stretched toward it from Claw's back.

Wham! The log smacked her hand, but she miraculously held on. Then, with both arms, she yanked the log out of the swirling water, clutching it tight as Claw moved them to shallow water.

"Giselle?! How are you are holding onto the log like that? The water is crazy strong," said Clare.

"I . . . am . . . crazy stronger!"

she exclaimed, jumping off Claw's back. "Oooof!" With a good grip on the log now, Giselle guided it toward shore.

Emmy ran and lifted Zee off. "You're safe, you're safe!" she cried as she wrapped him in her arms.

"Emmy!" whimpered Zee. He buried his head into her neck.

"Dad! Where is he?" said Giselle.

Clare scrambled up onto a boulder. "He floated downriver, but . . . I don't see him!" She looked around frantically for a way to get down to him. *Soar!* she thought. Her little eaglet was now a mighty eagle, larger than any bird Clare had ever seen. "C'mon!" she said as she leapt onto Soar's back.

"You think we can *fly* on her?" said Giselle.

"I think so!" said Clare.

"I'll stay with Zee," said Emmy.

"Okay, let's go, go, go!" Giselle jumped on behind Clare, and Soar took a few running leaps. Then, with one pull of her wings, she lifted into the sapphire-colored sky. As they rose above the churning river, the sun warmed their backs and they exhaled a breath they hadn't realize they'd been holding.

Framed by green, the muddy river twisted

and turned down the mountain. Soar banked to follow a bend and Clare cried out, "There's Dad!"

"Where?" Giselle said. "All I see are treetops!"

"I can see him—there, in that little inlet! He's not moving! Get us down, Soar!"

As Soar descended, Giselle finally spotted him. It looked like their father was lying on the inflated plastic bag in a quiet pool of water by the river's edge. His eyes were closed and his body was still.

"Dad!" cried Giselle. She jumped down and landed with a splash.

"Giselle?!" said the doctor, opening his eyes.

"Dad?!" cried Giselle. For the first time since Zee fell in the river, tears burned her eyes. "You weren't moving. I thought . . ."

"I was just resting. Gathering strength to hike back to you all," he murmured. But then he jumped up. "Zee! Where's Zee?"

Clare hopped off Soar. "Emmy's got him. He's okay, Dad. Don't worry." She wrapped her arms around him.

"Clare, you're safe, thank goodness," said Dr. J.A. as he struggled to his feet. "And . . . what are you girls wearing?"

"Long story. We'll take you to Zee—we can fly," said Clare as she turned him gently to face the eagle.

He gasped and fell back a step, but Giselle

steadied him. "That's our little Soar? I have so many questions, but right now we just need to get back. All together, and safe."

"*Caw!*" went Soar, and bowed her head. They hopped on her back and once again, she pumped her powerful wings and took to the sky.

CHAPTER 13

Emmy sat on the riverbank, stroking Zee's back. He kept his arms wrapped tightly around her, his head buried in her shoulder. Fluffy, now a full-sized powerful wolf, sat next to them, watching over his family. Claw, too, lay in the sun as it dried her enormous body. Emmy had explained to Zee that a lot of strange, magical things had happened that

day. But they would have to wait to find out why.

After Zee had rested and warmed up a bit, he looked at Emmy with red-rimmed eyes. "I'm sorry I ran for the mega-berries without you."

"Zee, all I care about is that you're safe." He hugged her tighter and a little sob escaped her throat. "And, *I'm* sorry that I let this happen."

Zee pulled her cheek against his head and rubbed her back with his little hand. Fluffy settled his head across their laps. They stayed that way for a while.

Finally, Emmy sat up and forced a smile. "That was super scary, but you're okay now. You have some scrapes and bruises, though. Can I take a look?"

He nodded.

Emmy gently inspected him. There were some nasty cuts, but thankfully, nothing seemed serious. "Buddy, you're okay. There's dirt in your scrapes, though. We should wash them off."

"No! It'll sting!" whined Zee.

"Maybe for a second. But then it will be over. C'mon." She walked Zee down to the river's edge. "Let's start here." She knelt and gently touched a large scratch on his leg. "Does it hurt?"

Zee gasped, but not because it hurt. When Emmy touched his skin, the cut closed up. It was instantly healed!

Zee stared at his sister. "Did you see that?!"

Emmy looked at her fingers in awe, then gently touched the other scrapes. They all healed, too, as if they'd never been there.

"AARRRROOO-RRR-RRR!" Fluffy bellowed into the sky.

"Whoa, Emmy. Look!" cried Zee.

Soar landed on the riverbank. After

climbing down, Clare, Giselle, and Dr. J.A. ran to Zee and Emmy. They shared a huge family hug.

"Zee, don't ever scare me like that again! Are you okay?" demanded Dr. J.A, looking his son up and down.

"I'm good, Daddy! I had cuts, but Emmy fixed them. See?"

"I don't see anything," said Dr. J.A, with a puzzled look. "Girls, what happened here today?"

Clare ran to the riverbank where they had left the trillium charm. She grabbed it and raised it over her head. "*This* happened, Dad!"

Dr. J.A. gasped at the trillium flower charm glowing magnificently in the late-afternoon sun. "What *is* that?!" he asked.

"It's our petal charms!" explained Emmy. "The ones you gave us this morning!"

"Impossible," said Dr. J.A. softly.

"I would have said that, too, Dad . . . *before*," said Giselle. "But when we needed to save Zee, our charms came alive, and combined!"

"Are they magic?!" asked Zee, eyeing the flower charm.

"We don't know," said Emmy. "But the charm *did* give us each a power."

"I became super strong," said Giselle.

"*That's* how you were able to swim against the current," said Dr. J.A.

"And I can see things really far away," said Clare.

"And Emmy has magic! In her fingers!" exclaimed Zee. He lifted her hands and stared at them as if he expected them to glow, too.

Clare cradled the glowing charm. "From petals to flower . . . are we sisters . . . with power?!"

Dr. J.A. truly didn't know. As a man of science, he didn't believe in magic. But he

also knew there were things in the universe that science couldn't explain. That didn't make them any less real.

Suddenly, there was a gurgle, and Zee clutched his belly dramatically.

"I'm starving!" he complained.

"Ahoooo!" agreed Fluffy.

"You know what? I haven't eaten all day, either!" said Dr. J.A.

"The strawberries," Giselle whispered to her sisters.

"Trillium pancakes are waiting at home," said Emmy.

"Plus an extra surprise," added Clare.

"Let's go," said Dr. J.A.

"Daddy, can I ride home with you?" asked Zee.

Dr. J.A. grinned. "You betcha!"

He lifted Zee onto Fluffy's back and then climbed onto Claw.

"Last one home is a rotten flower!" Zee called as the animals jogged up the trail.

"We still need strawberries for the suprise," said Giselle.

Woo! Woo! went Soar. She pointed her beak toward the top of the mountain.

Clare giggled. "Looks like Soar has an idea!"

The girls arranged themselves on the eagle's back,

pressing the flower charm tightly between their bodies. Soar glided close to the mountainside and dipped low enough for the girls to hold out their hands and pluck berries right off the vines. When they landed in the yard, each girl had two handfuls.

"That was a *berry* good ending!" said Clare.

"To one berry strange day!" Giselle laughed.

CHAPTER 14

Back at the tree house the girls took the stairs two at a time. They were halfway up when they heard *"Caw, caw!"* Soar stared at them from the grass. She was too big now to make it up the narrow stairs.

"I've got you," said Giselle. She raced into the family room, where she threw open the two huge glass windows.

Soar flew up, then tucked her wings and glided gracefully inside.

"Score! We beat Dad and Zee home!" said Giselle.

"I'll wash the berries," said Emmy.

"Should we change out of these . . . costumes?" said Clare. "I hate to take mine off." She twirled, and the pleats of her warrior outfit skirt opened to reveal different colors hidden within the pink fabric. She looked like a rainbow!

"Let's stay in our warrior wear!" said Emmy, takig a deep breath. "Mine smells so good! Just like the forest."

"This is so comfy, I may never take it off!" Giselle said. She tipped into a handstand

and walked on her hands. Her bright blue romper stayed perfectly in place, and the gold lightning bolts flashed as she moved.

"But, we need to wash up," She added once she landed back on her feet. "Race ya!" She was already heading for the ladder.

"Coming," called Emmy. "I'm just going to make sure everything is perfect for Dad."

She put the maple syrup and granola on the table. Then she placed the flower charm in the center, where it glowed like candlelight. *Hmmm . . . hadn't the glow been brighter at the river?*

Soar hopped to Emmy's side. She was so big now, she easily reached the tabletop.

"Caw, caw!" she went as she aimed her beak at the granola.

"Uh-uh, Soar," said Emmy. "We have to wait for the others."

As if on cue, Emmy heard the hose in the garden sputter.

"We're home!" called Dr. J.A. "Just washing up!"

The flower charm caught Emmy's eye again. The glow was definitely fading. And then, it flickered and went out completely! *Poof!* The individual charms pulled apart. Emmy gasped, then lifted her green petal charm from the table and stared at it.

There was another soft *poof!* and Soar shrank back down to mini'mal size. *"Squawk!"* she complained in her little voice. She couldn't reach the table anymore.

"Huh?" Giselle said as she and Clare descended the ladder. She was in her clothes from the morning, and so was Clare!

And Emmy was wearing her old clothes again, too.

Emmy looked at her sisters' shocked faces and then down at herself. "Oh, no!" she said.

"Does this mean our powers are gone, too?" Giselle wondered aloud. She bent her knees and strained to lift the kitchen table. It wouldn't budge.

"The magic must only last as long as the trillium charm stays together and glows," said Emmy.

"So . . . we have magic. . . . But only some-times?" Clare asked.

"Bull's-eye," said Giselle sadly.

Emmy frowned. Clare threw an arm

around her sister. "It's okay, Em. It just means we have to use the power wisely when we do have it."

"But when will that be? What if something bad happens again?" said Emmy. She sat down at the table and pointed the three charms toward one another, but none of the powerful pull from earlier was there.

"I don't think we can force the magic to happen," said Clare. "Today, the charms pulled toward each other when Zee was in terrible danger."

"So, the charms become magic in emergencies?" wondered Giselle aloud.

"I think so," said Clare. She handed her sisters their charms, and they each snapped them back into their jewelry. Emmy kept hers in her hand.

Just then, the kitchen door flew open and in ran Zee, followed by Fluffy and Claw. They were mini again, too!

"The magic is all gone!" whined Zee.

"For now," said Clare. She smiled at Emmy, but Emmy didn't smile back.

Emmy slipped out the kitchen door and sat on the last step, staring at the green charm. She turned it over and over in her hands.

"Em!" said Dr. J.A. "What are you doing out here all alone?"

"I wanted to give you this," she said softly. She handed her father the green charm.

"The magic only comes when there's an emergency."

"I see," said Dr. J.A. "But the charm is yours, honey, for whenever you need it." He tried to snap the charm back into her necklace, but she stopped him. "Em, what's wrong?"

"I don't deserve this charm!" she cried. "You said we were old enough, but look what happened today!" She hung her head and started to cry.

Dr. J.A. gently lifted Emmy's chin so he could look her in the eye. "Em, today was *not* your fault. Zee had a terrible accident. But that's all it was—an accident. No one is to blame."

"I told Zee to wait for me before he went on the bridge, but he didn't hear me!" cried Emmy.

"That happens even when *I* tell him things," said Dr. J.A. "Em, I'm so proud of you and your sisters. You used the charms to work together to save Zee! I can't think of any better proof that you're old enough to have them."

Emmy threw her arms around her dad. If he thought she was mature enough for the charm, maybe she was.

"Ready?" said the doctor as he stood up. He took the green charm and reattached it to her necklace.

"Ready," agreed Emmy. They walked hand in hand back into the house.

When they reached the kitchen the doctor's eyes fell on the beautiful table. "Look at those gorgeous trilliums!" he said. "They seem particularly appropriate today!"

"It goes with the breakfast we made for you!" said Clare.

"But it's dinnertime," said Zee.

"Well, the only thing I love more than breakfast for dinner is all of you!" said Dr. J.A. He spread his arms and the girls ran to him in a terrifically tight triplet hug.

"Dad, you are Just Awesome," said Giselle.

"We're so lucky you found us," said Emmy.

"Happy Founding Day!" said Clare.

Zee didn't say anything at all. He just ran full speed into the hug.

Ooof.

"Let's get this party started!" said Dr. J.A. "Who's up for hide-and-find before pancake supper?" The kids squealed with delight as they ran to hide.

Turn the page for a
sneak peek of the next
Trillium Sisters
adventure

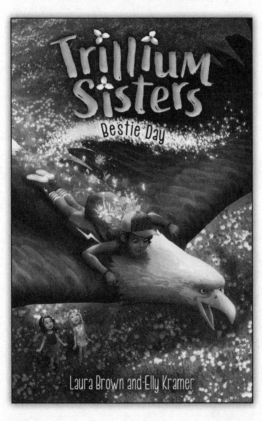

CHAPTER 1

As the morning sun poured into the tree house, Emmy, Giselle, and Clare looked through the bins in their craft room. It was Bestie Day, the holiday when everyone on Trillium Mountain celebrated their besties. As sisters *and* best friends, the triplets wanted to make one another perfect presents.

"Ugh," said Emmy. "Markers? Glitter

glue? Pipe cleaners? None of this feels special enough for Bestie Day gifts."

Giselle fiddled with the pet rocks they had made last year. "Yeah, we're eight now. This year, our gifts have to really rock!"

Clare giggled. "I know! Let's hike into the forest. We're old enough to go alone and there's tons of cool stuff there to use for crafts."

"Sounds fun," agreed Emmy. "But we still have to figure out exactly what we're making."

Clare tucked her hair behind a pink headband she had decorated with tiny flowers. It gave her an idea. "How about matching headbands? We can dress them up with pretty things we find, like I did with this one."

Laura Brown is an early childhood expert and has served as Content Expert and Research Director for Nick Jr., Disney Junior, Amazon Kids, DreamWorks Animation Television, PBS Kids, Universal Kids, and many others. She lives in Tenafly, New Jersey.

Elly Kramer has created and led the development of numerous award-winning TV shows, online games, and apps, and has produced and developed over thirty-five shorts. She served as Vice President of Production and Development with Nickelodeon. She lives in Los Angeles, California.